Stories of CAMP OAKWOOD

Written by Crew 160

Eliana Hutson
Madeleine Ha
Ruthie Gluck Feder
Samaya Dewan
Victoria Collett
Zoe Jovanovic White

Under the direction of Gary Rudoren and
Written Out Loud Studios

Cover design by Naomi Giddings

 **Written Out Loud**

ISBN 978-1-312-08954-9

This book is dedicated to all the loving parents and supporters of this crew, and to each other.

CHAPTER - VAL

Hello world or should I say dear diary...

Briiiiiiiiiiiing!!! Yay it was lunch and the last day of school for me, Valentine Simeone Lacker aka Val.

Now we get to go to camp and see our best friend, Sasha May Brown. I headed to my locker and put my books in it, shut it and ran off to the cafeteria. As soon as I got to the cafeteria my sister Catrina waved me over. I took my lunch and sat next to her.

"I can't wait to go to camp and spend time with Sasha," my sister cried. '

'Yeah, me too," I said. "So, on my list for packing I want PE clothes, camp uniform, and swimming trunk."

My sister said; "Mom said Sasha would come to our house and help pack."

"Oh, can we talk about PE?" Cat asked. I tuned her out right there. I started thinking about how me and my sister met Sasha. It all started on the first day of school in Westchester NY. We made friends in a flash and we went to camp and as we bonded more and more we became best friends but then something terrible happened. We had a little house in Westchester Woods, but then after pre-k we had to go to a city school so my parents got us a school in Manhattan. So now we only see each other during summer at camp.

"Earth to Val," my sister said, scaring me. "did you listen to anything I said?"

Later on diary!

I'm back!

***

Knock knock! Went the door as it does when people knock.

"Val, Cat, come on it's Sasha," their mom called from the door. My sister and I ran to the door.

"Hi guys," Sasha said," curls bouncing. "May I come in?"

"Sure," I said as me and Cat came in for a hug. We finally let go and led her upstairs to our bedroom.

"Wow," Sasha said as she took in the sight. There were shirts, pants, headbands, and socks of every hue. Cat's stuff was on her bed and mine on mine.

"Wow," she said again. There was silence and then we all just giggled. Then giggles turned to laughs and laughs turned to roars. Until I couldn't hear myself say, "ok mom's going to think we turned into giggling lions."

We laughed a little more and then Sasha finally asked, "Can I help with the packing?"

"Yes since Cat won't help I need some serious help," I said. Before Sasha could speak Cat cut her off, "what I can't help it if packings are not in my nature.

"Ha let's just pack ok sis," I said. We packed for three more hours. (because we had a clothing fight) Before we knew it there was a loud honk. That meant only one thing. "Camp bus!!!" We were off to a great summer at Camp Oakwood!

Hey Diary – it's me again later!

Time flew and pretty soon we were there. Me, Sasha, and Cat all squealed. It was the moment we'd been waiting for a year. We got off the bus and took in the sight. Camp

Oakwood was just as we remembered. With its cabins, tree-houses for the campers and all the trees, beautiful trees. Willow trees, pine trees, even the most rare kind of red wood. And of course, tons of Oak trees.

"I can't believe we are finally here" my sister said interrupting my thoughts.

"Look" Sasha said. She pointed to the big banner that said; "Sign-ups for HAMILTON musical".

"What does it say?" asked Cat. Cat could read - just not cursive.

"It says Sign up for Hamilton Musical" I answered "and you should totally try out Sash."

"I couldn't. The supporting roles are all boys and I don't want to be a boy."

"I'm not talking about a supporting role I'm talking about a lead!" I said in an obvious voice.

"Who would you want to be?" asked Cat.

"I want to be Angelica but......." whispered Sasha. "But you'll be totally amazing at Angelica," I said.

"You know what, I will audition" she said; "come on, we are cabin 12".

CHAPTER - JESSIE

Dear Diary,

I can't wait for my first day of my new camp! AHHH. I'm so excited! I wonder if there is a beach there? OH, or what if there is a pool!? This is too exciting. In some ways I'm scared. WHAT IF THEY DON'T HAVE A BEACH. I

WON'T BE ABLE TO SURF!! BUT WHAT IF THERE IS A BEACH BUT THERE ARE NO WAVES?

I'm starting to get very nervous.

Camps are supposed to be FUN. If it has no beach, it will be boring. UGHH! I'M SCARED. I'M SCARED. I'M SCARED...

Breathe, Jessie, BREATHE! I'm now excited I guess, but when I think about no beaches... AHHHH, I will be ok! I hope...

CHAPTER - SOPHIE

Dear Diary

I'm so worried and I'm almost at camp I AM SOOO EXCITED thought too. Well partly... my sister Alex is coming 🕸, BUT i am a Counselor and I hope to meet some other counselors like me. And won't be stuck with Alexis in town. She is so bossy, mom and dad are so happy that we are going to camp - they say that we need a break

BUT I think it's that they want a BREAK FROM US .

SOPHIE CALM DOWN they just need some relaxation time, come on just forget about it. Otherwise I hope there is a volleyball court and a swimming pool and ahhhh i want so much but i don't know if it is there I wish could know.

CHAPTER - OLIVIA

Dear Diary,

I just arrived at camp, I'm going to be a counselor! So, I obviously love kids. The cabin is like a treehouse except with clean water...it's kinda a luxury... oh wait, a luxury (cabin). I think there are going to be 2 or 3 other counselors. But at least I'll have a friend or 2! I was sunbathing at the pool 1 hour ago. It was really nice because nobody was there and I had the whole space to myself! Then suddenly someone my age-ish walked up to me and said; "Are you a counselor?"

I responded "uh... Yes. But first of all, who are you?"

"I'm Charlotte - call me Charli" she said.

It was 5:00 am. by then. 3 more hours till the kids come! They get out of the bus at 8:00am. and settle in their dorms for another hour. Then the day REALLY starts. You can tell I've been here before. 30 mins later... all the counselors start coming in, they're all like 14-19. Someone named Rosie took the top bunk... everybody was pretty frustrated. But while everyone was mad at Rosie, I called dibs on the other top bunk.

3 hours later, "The bus is here!!!" I squealed at the top of my lungs. We have 3 little girls that we share the dorms with and play with, it's basically the best job in the universe! Our little dorm mates are, Sasha, Valentine, and Cat. I think they are all 9. "56b!?" someone called from the bus.

"That's us!" Rosie, Chloe, Charlotte, and I said.

"I'll lead you to your bunks" I said. I led the girls through the main hall, through the offices, through the play pen and to the dorm 56b.

"Clothes go in the cabinets, swimming gear goes in the closet and information tag goes on the door nob, oh, and other luggage goes under the bunkbeds.

"C'mon" "Okay!" the girls answered. We went down the creaky ladder, through the ruffling grass, and then found Charlotte, Rosie, and Chloe.   "What do you girls want to do first?" all of us counselors said. "Water Slide" they responded.

"We should have known." Charlotte said with a big sigh.

"C'mon" I said "they're already going." 10 minutes later, we're at the water slides.

"The girls stepped up the very squeaky ladder {of course it was because of the water}. Such fun!

CHAPTER - CHLOE

Dear diary,

It's me, Chloe I am having sooooo much fun, I already told Rosie I want the top bunk, but she didn't listen. I haven't seen mom and dad for a year, all I have is Rosie, and she knows that. Boarding school was pretty fun the last day we even had a party! I am in the tiger bunk this year. I got a bit sick on the bus ride :(. Bye talk to you later:).

PS - soooo excited to be a counselor also happy they don't know who I am! Lol bye for reals now!

CHAPTER - SOPHIE

I'm back!

Dear diary, and I am here, at camp!

You know, I am so so excited and I am going to meet some other Counselor like me and I think their names are Charlotte, Rosie, Chloe, Olivia... well I THINK, hope they're nice.

CHAPTER - ROSIE

Dear diary,

Rosie here, I stole the top bunk from Chloe. I feel sooooooo evil I bet she is planning to get her revenge, lol. Can't wait to steal the first shower, I feel so devious. Oh no, I already feel sick to my stomach, I am a counselor now! Bye!

CHAPTER - SOPHIE

It's 1 Hour later aaaaaaaaaaaaaaaaaaaa I just ealized that i know NOTHING ABOUT BEING A COUNSELOR AAAAAAAAAAAAAAAAAAAAAAAA OMG WHAT AM I GOING TO DO?.............. ANSWER GOOGLE AAAAA they're taking people's phones .... quick google "how to be a Counselor????"

CHAPTER - CHARLI

Dear diary,

I love being normal, as well as at CAMP!!!!! Yeah, I know it's only the second day at camp but i have made a friend ALREADY!!!!!!

Her name is Olivia Maple, but she said I can call her Olivia. We made friends fast, or as i like to call it fast friends. She is really funny, and she said I was too. Here are some of her jokes:

What do you call a train carrying bubble gum?
A chew chew train!
Why did the M&M go to school?
Because it wanted to be a smartie!
Why couldn't the pony sing a lullaby?
Because he was a little horse!

Here are some of mine:
Why do bees have sticky hair?
Because they use honeycombs!
How do you throw a space party?
You planet!
What do you call a fake noodle?
An impasta!

Bye diary!!
I have to go, one of the campers is calling me.
Talk later! xxxxxxx

CHAPTER - JESSIE

HII, DIARY! It's me... AGAIN.

So you know I said "I'm so scared" WELL SCRAP THAT, IT'S SOOO FUN. The beach is so great. IT HAS GIANOR-MOUS WAVES EEEEK.. But i haven't made any friends, oh well! I SHOULD be eating right now but instead I'm writing in this diary.

Wait one sec I'm getting a burger and salad.

Back! It's 7:00 and we are going to watch a movie called Soul, never heard of it.

I GOT TO GET OFF, BYE!

CHAPTER - CHLOE

Heyyyyyy. It's me Chloe I'm soooooo excited for art class! I can't wait I'm gonna be the one in the center of the art hall! I'm soooooo excited . The auditions also sound fun. I'm pretty sure they are doing Hamilton. I'M NOT THROWING AWAY MY SHOT (to be in the center of the gallery. Bye, talk to you later:)

CHAPTER - ROSIE

What's up? Ohhh yeahhh you're only a diary you can't talk anyway - it's me, your ONLY FRIEND (i hope), Rose Meredith Williams, for some reason today i feel soooo fancy, maybe because the auditions are today for "THE BIG SHOW"

I think it's Hamilton? Maybe it is, maybe it isn't. I mean of course I'll get the lead right? I mean it's in my blood! But there is also Chloe and Charlotte so, maybe not. I can't wait to be from the 1700s!

THIS, has been Rosie.

PS -. I'm trying to do a cool goodbye, like Chloe does. I may or may not have read her diary.

CHAPTER - SOPHIE

HEY DIARY! I JUST MET THE COOLEST KIDS!!

CHAPTER - OLIVIA

Omg! Second day at camp! The showers are so nice and warm, usually i take a **cold** shower in the summer, but yesterday it was awfully cold!? Oh, did i mention that the beds were rock hard! I mean like finally, it's not like i'm sinking in a mattress. Yes if anybody will read my diary, they think i'm silly for thinking that rock hard beds are comfortable.

So some counselors are arriving tomorrow. Correct me diary one counselor is coming tomorrow. And my boss said that i can be the counselor of water! Including: pools, water slides, water park, ect.

Let's move from this subject. Okay obviously everybody i met is my friend. But I met a new friend, and her name is Charli short for Charlotte. She's **_great_** at making jokes. Plus, campers are super-duper cute.

CHAPTER – CHARLI

Today are AUDITIONS for the camp play, and everyone is excited about HAMILTON. But before we decided on who would be playing what, we had to decide who would be the judge/director and deciding that went a little like this:

All the bunks had a camp meeting and Rosie & I put it to order.

"OK CAMP OAKWOOD I call this meeting to order " Rosie said (I think that was a LITTLE much but...)

"So, we need a director but i don't want it or any of you, because you might be biased or mad. Also you're supposed to have fun not be stressed out by managing it so... So, from the counselors who wants to be director? I asked.

Five seconds later I was the only one with my hand up.

So, I guess that is that. Rosie said awkwardly.

"Yeah" I said, equally awkward.

Later I was taking a little walk when I heard "I challenge you to a   PRANK WAR!"

For what what... oh tots I'm definitely gonna win!!"

girls, girls i said. Stop making up PRANK WARS. That is a bad influence on our campers.

My mom would be proud of me. I thought she was always telling me to be ready for the star life.

GOSH Charli you sound like a businesswoman Olivia and Rosie said at the same time.

They looked at each other and broke into laughter. Hey as director of the HAMILTON I've been practicing some Hamilton jokes and wanna hear one?

"Ok" Olivia said.

"Sure" Rosie responded.

Ok here it goes :

Hamilton says; "Hey. George, knock knock."
Washington says; "Son, I do ot have time for this."
Hamilton: "C'mon. Knock knock."
Washington sighs; "Who's there?"
"Nacho"
"Nacho who"
"I'm nacho son!"

"Huh huh you like it?" I asked.
They burst out in a fit of laughter
"WHAT WHAT WHAT WHAT SHOULD I CHANGE
TELLLLLLMEEEEEEE"
"Ok ok" Rosie said "wellllllllllllllllllllllllllllllllllllllllllllllllllllllllll "
"Never mind Rosie"
"Hey!"
"That was great Charli "
"Thanks" I say
Ohh bye gotta go Lulu is calling me
Talk later alligator :)

CHAPTER - OLIVIA

HI! THERE'S AN AUDITION! So, I'm obviously going to audition for the camp play.... Drum roll please!! HAMILTON!! OMG! I know.... I auditioned for Eliza, and it's tomorrow! OKAY I AM HAMILTON OBSESSED! Ok, here are the cast members I THINK: Rosie: HAMILTON, Me: ELIZA HAMILTON, Sasha: ANGELICA, Alex: PEGGY, Jessie: THOMAS JEFFERSON, LuLu: AARON BURR, LAST Cat: KING GEORGE! But… Me and Rosie are disagreeing on who's going to be Eliza. So I'm going to challenge her to a PRANK WAR!!

30 mins later… "I'm definitely gonna win Rosie" I say "I challenge you to a PRANK WAR!" "For what… oh tots I'm in!!" She responded. She obviously knows that I'm talking about being Eliza. Then Charli busted in.

I said "Gosh Charli, you sound like a business woman!" But, something she didn't know was that I'd already set up a prank… Flashback: 10:37 pm. I snuck into the bunk Rosie was sleeping in, took her chair, and put a water balloon on the chair. Put the chair under the desk and BOOM! The prank was finished!

8:30 am. Rosie wakes up (of course I was already awake! But I was in bed cause I didn't want to look sus. Here's the story… 8:31 am. Rosie gets out of bed. Puts on her clothes. Then she walks to her desk to watch some videos that her family sent her. She sat down and the water spilled all over her pants. "OLIVIA! IM GONNA GET YOU BACK!!!! She yelled.

Bye, bye gotta go!.....

CHAPTER - CHLOE

Hi again... I just wanted to tell you on some information. Rosie did another prank on me. When I was getting out of the shower, Rosie put shaving cream in my shoes.

Then I had to take another shower. But one thing was funny, when I was playing tennis with Rosie she had a rainbow tennis racket.

"Rainbows are for babies", I said.

"No they aren't!" said Rosie

"Then prove that rainbows are not for babies."

"Now that you aren't talking I can actually, thankfully, luckily prove that rainbows are for babies. Fhgufueywfhiehguhrlh. Sorry, I'm just crazed out because tomorrow are auditions! I need to be Eliza. You know I need to because I ABSOLUTELY NEED to beet ROSIE!!!!!!!! She keeps insisting that she's gonna win, and if she wins... that will be unacceptable!!!!!

CHAPTER - ROSIE

Uuuuuuuhhhhhh hi. I don't really have much to say though. Ohhhh yeeeeaaahhh

Chloe started a prank war, I filled her shower shoes with shaving cream hahhahhaha. I know it's bad but hear me out okay? she said that "my racket was a rainbow and, rainbows are for little kids!"

oh wait she's stepping in the shower gotta go!

14

CHAPTER - OLIVIA

HI!!!!!!! Ok I know your all in to hear about the PRANK WAR!!!! OMG! I didn't tell you the camp's name yet. It's Camp Oakwood!

Ok..... Now back to the PRANK WAR!!!!!!!!

Flashback... Monday 2:oopm.

"OLIVIA! COME HEAR!" said Rosie.

"What do you need......" I said.

"Let's eat!" She said,

"Ok...But first play this game called blank face." said Rosie. I know, SOOOO SUS.

"OK???" I responded.

"The Instructions are to read the message then pick a different message and do that."

"Go on, pull the tabs out!" she said. I pulled it out.

"What does it say?"

"It says...I'm stupid not smart ."

"SAY IT!!" "I"M STUPID< NOT SMART AND WEIRD!" I obviously said that as fast as I could.

"What does the other tab say?"

"Uhhhhh.... Slap a whipped cream pie on your face. "DO IT!!!!"

"FINE..." Several minutes later... Rosie walks back to the dorm. Sorry I cut out the best part, but I cut it out for a reason. I cut it out because I don't want to remind myself of the weird laugh Rosie has... It's like CREEPY.

TTYL (Rosie's coming)
Sincerely, Olivia the gggrrreeeaaatttt...........!!!!!!!??????

***

Hi again... I just wanted to tell you on some information. Rosie did another prank on me. When I was getting out of the shower, Rosie put shaving cream in my shoes. Then I had to take another shower. But one thing was funny, when I was playing tennis with Rosie she had a rainbow tennis racket.

"Rainbows are for babies", I said.

"No they aren't!" said Rosie

"Then prove that rainbows are not for babies."

"Now that you aren't talking I can, thankfully, luckily prove that rainbows are for babies. Fhgufueywfhiehguhrlh. Sorry, I'm just crazed out because tomorrow are auditions! I need to be Eliza. You know I need to because I ABSOLUTELY NEED to beet ROSIE!!!!!!! She keeps insisting that she's gonna win, and if she wins... that will be unacceptable!!!!!

CHAPTER - JESSIE

Hello diary, I'm auditioning for the play hehe. It's Hamilton. I want to get Angelica, everyone is auditioning for Eliza.

I know she's great, but I won't get her. ALL THE GIRLS WANT HER!! It's annoying "noo I'm going to get her and marry Alexander Hamilton" "noo me"

LIKE WHO CARES, AUDITION FOR PEGGY, ANGELICA, OR ENSEMBLE, I'M MAD because then we won't have other characters cause all the girls want ELIZA. Heh, i got little too mad about that. I'm probably going to be a dance choreographer if I don't get it.

I won't get it.

I'm stage frightened, anyways... going to skateboarding. BYE!

CHAPTER - ROSIE

Dear diary,

OMG! Sooooo guess who was judging the auditions... Minnie Mylie! You know, that girl from Hollywood who was a tiny bully! And for some reason she hates me now!

No chance I'm getting the lead now! Luckily there was another judge, a better judge, her name was Charlotte she is one of my fellow counselors Chloe is currently out supervising art and doing it too.

Oh! Here comes Charlotte! Bye! THIS has been Rosie.

CHAPTER - ROSIE

Ommmmmmmmmgggggggggggg! I auditioned.

CHAPTER - CHLOE

Dear diary,

I get to supervise art! Eeeeeeeeekkkk i'm sooooo excited! And I'm even allowed to paint! And maybe even

17

get a chance to be in in the center of the art hall!

Yay! Okay sooooo Rosie says that MINNIE MYLIE IS BACK! I hated her sooooo much she used to be my BFF before I found Rosie. I'm glad I switched. See u later :)

CHAPTER - CHARLI

Dear DIARY,

I really can't choose between Rosie and Olivia to be ELIZA. I want to choose Rosie because her acting is spot-on-(then choose Rosie- wait I am not finished!) But as i was saying before Diary rudely interrupted me I want to choose Olivia because her voice is beautiful.

But anyway, we i mean ME ROSIE OLIVIA JESSIE SAHSA AND VAL AND CAT AND ALEX

We're having a singing contest it was alot of fun. Val, Cat, Chloe, were the judges. And they said my voice was rich and melodic i got a ten out of ten oh wait did i say that there were doing to be 3 rounds so that there were going to be eliminations... i went to all 2 rounds at the third round i was just me and Rosie.

What song am i singing i asked

Wrecking ball and as for u Rosie Titanium

Rosie started when she finished we all burst into applause

I hadn't realized earlier what I was against

CALM DOWN CHARLI IT'S SUPPOSED TO BE A FRIENDLY COMPETITION!

It was my turn I sang my heart out

And the said the winner is............................
CHARLI!!!!!!!!!!!!!

Congrats

Yay for you

Sorry Rosie the song we picked for u might not have been the best fit

Its ok don't worry its ok

Bye got to go have dinner the bell just rang

More later

P.S. i think it was Rosie's turn to ring the dinner bell

P.P.S. OLIVIA IS TOMMOROW

P.P.P.S. JESSIE IS DAY AFTER

P.P.P.P.S. I AM DAY AFTER

P.P.P.P.P.S. BYE-BYE FOR REAL NOW

CHAPTER - ROSIE

Dear diary,

There was a singing competition and they were three rounds I made it to the last round against Charli I sang Titanium and she sang Wrecking Ball, but she won - the judges said, "and the winner is...Charli. I'm sorry Rosie, but we just think it wasn't the right song for you"

I really think they know ties are boring and we're just trying to make it interesting anyway I get to ring the Dinner bell I heard someone baking a nap ha ha Ha and I'm pretty sure it's Olivia bye!

CHAPTER - VAL

Dear Diary

"I CAN'T!!!!!!!" shouted Cat.

"Come on, just one more thing," I said. I quickly unpacked all my things and started helping Cat.

"AHHHHHHHHHHHHHHHH" said a voice that was so loud and high pitched it almost made me pee in my pants, almost. Sasha burst through the door so fast. if a normal person did it, they would have looked sloppy but not Sasha she bust through that door like a gazelle.

"I got the part!" She said so loud she practically screamed. We immediately dropped what we were doing and ran to give her the biggest bear hug ever. We had convinced her to AUDITION for Angelica and she took it.

"I told you you would," I said! Then I had the greatest idea OF MY LIFE, WE SHOULD DO SOMETHING MEANINGFUL AND HELP SASHA at the play. I smiled. It was going to be a long day.

CHAPTER - JESSIE

Ok well, I got Thomas Jefferson which I'm pissed off about, LIKE ITS NOT A BIG PART AND WHY THE HECK WOULD I GET A BOY. I'M ABOUT TO KILL AND WHEN I SAY KILL I MEAN KILL WHOEVER THE HECK DID THE CASTING!! ILL DO IT, FINE! BUT YEAH LEMME JUST GO TELL SOME PEOPLE.

I'M BACK I TOLD THE COUNSELORS, they said keep

it please, Jessie. I'll do it, I'll do it but I WONT be happy, ok? IM RIGHT NOW CRYING IN MY BUNK. JUST GIVE LIKE KEVIN OR LUKA THE PART.

Bye):

CHAPTER - CHARLI

Dear diary,

I just got a postcard from my best friend Vivian back at home.

I read it five times before I finally put it away.

Then I went to the pool to relax for a little while. Olivia and Rosie and Chloe had the same thought apparently because they were all playing in the deep end.

'Hey guys'' I called HHHHHHHHHHIlIllllllllllllllllllllllllllllllllll CHARLOTTE they yelled back

We played for about 1000 seconds before Jessie came over deep in conversation. From what i heard they were looking for the beach

"Hey Jessie" I called.

Their heads quickly turned.

Wow I thought quick reflexes

The beach is the other way which I'm pretty sure u were looking for since you have yr surfboards.

"Quick fun fact" I said "I am a really good surfer too"

Jessie grinned "I challenge you to have a surfing contest"

Game on.

Luckily i had my surfboard handy. Ten min later I was riding a wave in the lead and thought I had won because I was like 7 feet from the beach. Just then Jessie zoooooooooom past me and made it to the beach.

one minute later

Jessie was lying down on her towel reading a book looking like she had been there for hours with a smug smile on her face.

I look 11 inches away and there was Rosie

"Tied" we yelled at the same time.

Then our attention turned back to Jessie

"I win" she said smugly "what do I get?"

"Uhhhh what do u want?"

"Our dessert for the next two nights."

She shook her head

There goes that idea I was hoping she would say yes because i would ask the director if we could have coffee crumble cake and pastries for the next two days, because Jessie does not like ether of those so we wouldn't have to give her our dessert.

I really am an evil genius.

Bye gotta go it's my turn to ring the dinner bell

Talk later

CHAPTER - ROSIE

Aaaaaa I'm sssooooooaaakkking wet! I just finished a surf race with Jessie and Charli sooooo here's the story. I was chilling in the pool with Olivia and then Charli walked up to us and asked if she could join, Jessie was looking for the beach she came with a book and a surfboard 5 minutes later she was curled up looking like she was there for hours. Ten minutes or so later she went to keep finding the beach Charli challenged her to a surf battle and asked if I could join she said yes

On our way there I started to explain the rules, i said "so here's the rules if you fall off a wave paddle back whoever gets back first without falling is the winner and the two losers take the winner's chores for a whole week!"

Once the race started, I caught a big wave, it slowed me down but it was fun! Of course, the winner was Jessie, "the surfing pursuit" as I like to call her. I was so unlucky because one of her chores was cleaning the toilet!

Bye!

CHAPTER - JESSIE

Rosie and Chloe and Olivia are having a prank war. It's pretty dumb, right? They are 2 girls in my bunk. Anyway, at skateboarding, I got excluded by the boys,

AGAIN, I'm seriously the only girl there! I get aggressive, they should STAY AWAY. OH, I FORGOT TO SAY THE MOST IMPORTANT PART OF MY DAY.... THERE IS A SURFBOARDING COMPETITION WITH CHARLIE AND ROSIE! I'm totally gonna win it. Charlie and Rosie you going down badddd.

I GTG TO PRACTICE SORRYYY BYEEE!

CHAPTER - CHLOE

Ummmmmmm... I have nothing to say so I just want to note that our bunk's team color for color war is... GOLD! Which means number one baby!

hi! i was assigned the head of the set painting! yayyyyy! I heard Rosie and Olivia are having a prank war idk why though. Nothing else is that exciting bye!

CHAPTER - VAL

Dear Diary,

"What?" said Cat as she scored. Cat and I were talking but she had insisted on playing soccer so now I was **watching** her.

I said, "I think we should help with the play!"

Cat said annoyed. "There's no way I'm playing some fancy pants person that is not me! And that is final," Shouted Cat.

"I know," I said. "You do?"

"Then why are you asking me!" I sighed "because I'm talking about backstage help."

"Oh, that makes more sense," she realized. "I'll do it"

"Anything for Sasha" she announced. "Then come on, we're late" I screamed, and we ran like the wind all the way to Sasha.

CHAPTER - SASHA

Dear diary,

Val always writes in her diary so I'm deciding why not me? Hi, it's me, Sasha and something amazingly crazy happened today! Well, you probably want to know. Oh, do you think my handwriting is just amazing, way better than Val's, not that I've seen or read her diary......... Oh sorry yep, yeah, and yes, I do trail off a lot....

Sorry, nervous. Ok here goes, I was at rehearsal for Hamilton... yes Hamilton I got the part of Angelica Skyler when my director asked if I could go get a prop from backstage. So, I said yes and skipped all the way to the place beyond the scenes when I bumped into Val.

"WHAT, WHAT, AND WHAT" I said my lips twisting into such a giant smile my jaw started throbbing. I gave her a huge bear hug.

"We wanted to help out," she said.

"We" I asked. "Cat, come on" she urged me. I came along and saw Cat. We all hugged...... But then again. I read Val's diary, so this was not as much of a surprise.

I smiled. "Gotta go" I said "Charlotte is gonna kill me" -Sasha

CHAPTER - JESSIE

There was a surfing competition, ofc, i won. I'm the best at sports. My bunk girls must now clean my room! I don't really have time to write in my diary anymore. I'm busy. So yeah i gtg to waterfront!

Sorry! Never mind never mind. I'm going to ask the girls to stop cleaning, they're like teasing me like "Oh master" or "please forgive me your highness!" I kinda even feel bad for u guys.

CHAPTER - CHARLI

Dear diary,

Ugh, I really hate cleaning the toilet, it's the worst.

Once when I was cleaning it i got so disgusted that i actually threw up in it. I know not very grown up like but i couldn't help it.

Anyway all this talk is making me want to PUKE!!!!!!!

TURN PAGE *TURN PAGE* *TURN PAGE*

AHH a fresh page to talk about something new.

Ok so I'm really stressed like crazy stressed. Olivia and Rosie came at me like lightning Olivia said her parents could only come on night but Rosie said the same thing

"This is great" I said

"On Olivia's parents night Olivia will be Eliza"

"Duh"

"And on Rosie's parents night she"

"We get in we get it"

"So Olivia are your parents coming first night or second night"

"Second."

"Hey that's my parents night" Rosie protested

Ugh and i thought we had found the perfect solution #sadface

#annoyedface

#madface

"What about we change while intermission" Olivia suggested

No i said that won't work I'll check in on u in five i have to see how the props and backgrounds are going.

Ok

FIVE MINUTES LATER

Hey girl

Hey great news my parents have to go to my brother's soccer game and so there coming on the second night Olivia revealed

Great

Woooooooohooooo

And that's how we solved the mix op mystery

bye gotta go get a frog to put in Rosie's bed

CHAPTER - CHLOE

Hi! I got a letter from my parents that I really want to read to you here it is:

Dear Chloe,

We have amazing news for you! You have a sister! Well, you will. Your real mother is still alive and she had another child, she is expected to be born in late August, we really wish we could tell you how she is still alive but it is very hard to explain we started directing movies a month ago and now we are on a time crunch, so we will send a letter explaining it all soon. And if you're wondering yes, your baby sister will be joining the family and her name will be, Abigail and of course you call her abbe for short we miss you so much!

Love,
Your mom and dad, Susan and Bill love you!

OOOMMMMMMMGGGG! I'm getting a baby sisssss I can't wait to meet Abigail! I HAVE to go tell Rosie! Bye!

CHAPTER - ROSIE

Dear diary,

Good news, Chloe has a new baby sis and is going to play with Balie! Oh yeah I forgot that you are my new dairy and I just got you last month Anyway Balie was born five months ago soooo that's it for now bye!

CHAPTER - CHLOE

I forgot to say that the letter I got was from a while ago because it's a camp Oakwood tradition to only get mail on Sunday because everyone will get mail, and here is the second letter,

Dear Chloe,

Here is the story about your mother, she couldn't afford to raise you as her own and we love you oh so much and your father died soon after you were born we love you so much goodbye!

Love,
Mom and Dad

CHAPTER - ROSIE

Dear diary,

Olivia's parents messed up; they actually can only come the second night because her brother has a soccer game the first night! Anyway I have to go rehearse bye!

CHAPTER - CHLOE

Dear diary,

I really want to find out more about my real mom and dad now! There is sooooo much more to discover! Anyway I need to go watch Rosie's rehearsal, sooooooo bye!

CHAPTER - ROSIE

Dear dairy,

My mom called and said she could only come on the first night because she had a big schedule for people to audition for her and dad's new movie, it's called "The Darkness Within" but same with Olivia's parents!

Oh! I gtg bye!

CHAPTER - CHLOE

Dear diary,

I finished painting sets! So now I can focus on the center of the art hall. I painted a sunset at the Eiffel Tower! Bye!

CHAPTER - JESSIE

Well, I guess I have rehearsals for Hamilton today! I really don't wanna do it!! Wait a sec... brb.... I'M GOING TO CRY.

So, i told the director i didn't wanna do it and she was like "no!, who will be Thomas?"

I was like "UHH IDK? NOBODY!" and then she was like, "Well.. WELL, um" and then I was like "LISTEN, i don't wanna play him! So pls, let me be. I don't have to be in the play... I also got teased for getting that part at the skating park and- and, ITS JUST NOT FAIR!"

Oh! and, not to mention, I got punishments for being "mean" and the girls in the other bunks were LAUGH-ING AT ME! SHUT UP! MIND YOUR OWN BUSINESS!!!! Umm so yeah...

I will now write a letter TO MY MOM! Here it is,

Hi, MOM! Thanks a lot for signing me up for Oakwood Camp. Im having suuuuuuch a great time. NOW LET ME LEAVE. WE DO CHORES AND KIDS AND COUNSLERS ARE MEAN, AND THEN I GET NAMED THE BULLY!! I GOT LAUGHED AT FOR GETTING THOMAS JEFFERSON IN THE SCHOOL PLAY, HAMILTON (the overrated Broadway show.) JUST LET ME LEAVE, OK?

CHAPTER - OLIVIA

Hi again! Today I have *some* news. Jessie got in trouble!! OMG!

So sad for her. Here's the story... Flashback... 2:37 p.m. Jessie was crying in her bed but still writing in her diary. I mean, give a clap. That's some *good* multitasking. Ok back to the story. She was crying in bed.

"Hi!" I said. "Is everything Ok???"

"No... I got kicked out, we're moving, my dog died, my mom's in the hospital!" she said all fastly.

"Tell me why you got kicked out!" I said cheerfully.

"Well... I really didn't want to be Thomas Jefferson, so I asked the director and she said then who's gonna be him? I tried to think of something, but nothing came out. But please.... I absolutely can't be Thomas, I said. You absolutely have to. Then i started saying I just couldn't be him. Then I said that I challenged her to fight. We started fighting. Obviously she won. But I got kicked out. Even though *I was* the bleeding *I* was the one who got kicked out." said Jessie

"Oh, Ok" I said. 'Why don't I leave you alone."

By Diary! T.T.Y.L!
Love olivia$maker

CHAPTER - CHARLI

MORE PROBLEMES!!!!!!!!!!!!!!!!!!!!!!!!

NOW MY NEW PROBLEM IS WHO WILL PLAY THOMAS JEFFERSON

I CAN'T TAKE IT ANYMORE...... TOMMOROWS OPENING NIGHT AND NOW WE DON'T HAVE A THOMAS JEFFERSON

OH AND TO TOP IT OFF I GOT INTO A WORD FIGHT WITH JESSIE AND HAD TO GIVE JESSIE A BIG SCOLDING AND TOLD HER SHE CAN'T SAY MEAN AND HURTFUL THINGS TO THE OTHERS AND THAT HER PUNISHMENT WOULD BE

1. SHE HAS TO DO HER WHOLE BUNKS CHORES
2. SHE CAN'T GO TO WATERPARK TIME
3. SHE HAS TO PLAY THOMAS JEFFERSON

AND IF SHE DOESN'T DO A GOOD JOB ON THOSE THREE THEN

4. I MIGHT TELL HER PARENTS

I feel really bad now

I'm going to the camp shop to get some candy and flowers for her. Maybe I will get a card ......

Gotta go bye

CHAPTER - OLIVIA

Hi! So today I have a couple things to talk about.... One: There's a mix-up about the show!

Two: My mom called me a said that we're moving after camp!!!!!

THE MIX-UP!!!! 10:35a.m. I hear the phone ringing. It was for me.

"Hello?" I said how may I help you?"

"Hi Honey-Bun" It was my mom!

"Hi mom!" "What do you want?"

"I just wanted to say that Julian (annoying little brother), dad (dad), And I (mom) are going to see the Hamilton movie or play. Whatever you call it. On Saturday!" said mom. "YAY!!!!!!!!" I said. "NOOOOO!!!" Rosie busted in. "Why Not?" "Cause my fam (family) is coming that day."

"Oh No" I said. "The plan is not going to work!" "I know!" said Rosie. At that point I'd already hang up the phone.

The Plan.....! So I was talking about the plan that we had. So, I'll tell you about that right now. Flashback...Yesterday 1:30 p.m. Rosie and I were talking about how we were both going to play Eliza.

"How bout we change..." I said

"Never mind" I said again.

"How bout we do you do one night I'll do the other." Rosie said. "Great!" But now that "THE MIX-UP" Happened I had come up with a better idea.

33

"How bout we switch during intermission!" I very smartly said. "Actually, my mom was mistaken and said Saturday!"

"No Problem" I said.

THE MOVING PART!!! Flashback.... 10:40 p.m. "ring ring" I hear the phone saying.

"Hello how can I help you, What do you need?" I said.

"Uh... can I talk to Oliva Maple?" said the person.

"Speaking" I said.

"Hi, It's Mommy!"

"Hello! BTW I call you *mom* now."

"Oh, Right"

"So what were you talking about?"

"We're moving to N.Y.C!!!!" "YYYYYYY!!!!!YEAH!!!!!!-YEAHHHHH!!!!"

I said; "Bye I gotta go to sleep."

"Bye, Love you!"

Now I actually gotta go to sleep.!? Bye!!!

Hi. My mom called me and now they're coming on Sunday. Only because my brother Julian has his tryouts.

CHAPTER - CHLOE

Dear diary,

I loved watching everyone from backstage! My mom and dad always said "I was made for stage" even though I only liked to paint. We also had our campfire I didn't speak because I like to lay low TTYL!

CHAPTER - ROSIE

Dear diary,

I just got back from Hamilton! IT WAS AWESOME! I felt like I could belt till the day was out! Anyway after that we had the annual final campfire. I helped lead it and we all made speeches here was mine " I loved being with everyone here at Camp Oakwood!

I loved being a counselor at Tiger bunk! I will hope to see all of you next year!" Did you like my speech?! Bye I need to pack you up now.

CHAPTER - CAT

Dear Book, I'm Catrina, Cat for short. It's my first time writing in a diary, that's what Val calls it at least. Back to the point, so take it easy on me.

Anyway I'm writing to say how AMAZING the play was with Sasha, pretty sets, cool costumes, pretty sets, and petty sets. To say but not to brag. I made pretty sets. Oh, fine if you really want to know. Sasha was beautiful. She sang with so much passion and acted with so much enthusiasm, even I loved it.

My favorite was satisfied, you know like" I toast to the groom" -that one. Anyway, she was so amazing.

CHAPTER - JESSIE

Ok! I got this new purple marker, I like it. Anyway, I finished my punishments. Yay?

Umm... at least i did punishments instead of being Thomas. Also, everyone has friends, me? NOPE! I try and try and try and yeah I get no friends.

I AM HAPPY I AM LEAVING. ITS AUGUST AND I'M READY TO LEAVE THIS PLACE! LET ME PACK, ONE SEC. YEEEEEEEEEEEEEEE!!!! I PACKED, yay, I'm now walking to the bus... I'm here on the bus, it's been 15 minutes? 20? Idk. OH JEEZ HELP ME. ermm.. I gagged. I. CAN'T. WAIT. TO. GET. HOME. YAYYYYYYYYYYYYYYYYYYYYYYYY!!!!!

Let me catch my breath. Sorry I'm so excited, well.... Bye!

CHAPTER - CHARLI

OMG I CAN'T BELIEVE THE PLAY IS OVER!!!!!!!!! !!!!!!!!!!!!!!!!!!!!!!!!

And every one was so good i am so proud gosh I'm really turning into my mother (she always drops tear or two after any production) but back to my drama witch i think is more interesting

So, Jessie did a good job on her punishments, so I didn't tell her parents. Oh and Jessie told me why she didn't want to be Thomas Jefferson, its because she got teased at the roller skating park for playing a boy\man in the play.

I was walking by the other day and i saw her taking out the garbage

Uggggg i feel sorry for her

Anyways i don't have so much time to write so I'll move on to my next topic . we had a last day of camp-campfire and we told spooky stories sing songs and eat s'mores it was the best

I MEAN THE BEST

I really am glad i became a counselor because i made a lot of new friends campers and counselors

Gotta go

CHAPTER - CHLOE

Dear diary,

I CAN'T BELIEVE MY PARENTS LIED TO ME THIS WHOLE TIME! Sorry, when I get back to New York I can't wait to meet my real mom! We are visiting her art gallery, well... have you ever heard of Sophia Davis, that's her! Anyway I loved camp this summer! TTYL!

CHAPTER - ROSIE

Dear diary,

We are on the bus right now. I really want to talk to Chloe because she feels like her parents lied to her into thinking her mom had passed from giving birth to her. I can't wait to come back next year. I'll talk to you when I get home...

CHAPTER - OLIVIA

Hi! Today I have *some* things to talk about. It's the last day of camp! I know so crazy that it already happened! 1. I just finished the Hamilton plays. It was *crazy* hard for me and Rosie because we needed to memorize 2 parts! Hamilton and Eliza. Well, let's stop talking about the crazy past. Let's talk about the chilling future!

2. Today we also got to do a campfire (the director thought of it)! It was so crisp in the camping area. We got to sing songs and tell stories. I told the story of toys coming to life (I'll tell you the story later). And we sung... who knows what the song is called.

3. The story is a bit creepy. I'm just gonna re-cap because the story is *super **duper*** long. Once upon a time there was a girl named June. She liked her name accept when the month June struck. Everything started changing, her mom started suffering, her teachers started being mean, everyone forgot about her birthday, but most of all... she turned into a teddy bear. Read more to learn about all the adventures and suffers that June has.

bbbbbbyyyyyyeeeee
I'm gonna be late for the bus! Once I'm on the bus we'll talk again!

CHAPTER - CHARLI

Dear diary,

Hey, I am at my house on the west side and a crazy thing happened a couple of hours ago that I felt I needed to tell u

OMG i can't believe I live TWO buildings away from Olivia.

Ok so heres what happened; Olivia and i were sitting together on the bus then i said hey where do u live then i will write to you and we will be pen pals

So, she said she lives at The Starlight apartment, Zipcode: 99915 Number of the building: 312 on the west side

"OMG, OMG!" I said. "I live 2 buildings away!"

"I live in The Majestic, Zipcode: 99915 Number of building: 325 on the west side

Anyway, i have to go to dinner now but i just wanted to tell u that.

Anyway, times two it's so cool right

Ohh my mom's calling me

Bye

CHAPTER - SOPHIE

I really had a better summer than I imagined. Prank wars, musicals, and funny kids - I can't wait to come back!

CHAPTER - OLIVIA

Hi! Back from the bus a crazy happened a couple of hours ago. Me and Charli were talking and then she suddenly asked, "Where are you moving?"

I said "The Starlight apartment, Zipcode: 99915 Number of the building: 312" "OMG, OMG!" Charli said. "I live 2 buildings away!" "I live in The Majestic, Zipcode: 99915 Number of building: 325"

Bye! It's sooo cool right!!!

CHAPTER - VAL

Dear Diaries. It's me Val, I loved this summer. My favorite part was, well... everything. From beginning to end. This was a great summer because I was with the girls And that's something that will never change.

CHAPTER - CAT

Hi, it's Cat. I really liked this summer. My favorite part was all the sports and painting sets, I really made lots of new friends, and of course I loved spending time with Sasha and Val. I also totally agree with Val.

CHAPTER - SASHA

It's Sasha. Val and Cat have covered a lot of amazing things about this summer and there is just one more thing.

My favorite part was the play because I never would have been in it if Val had not convinced me to do it and never gotten. anything and so will I for them. That's what keeps our friendship strong.

We are always there for each other and that will never change, so happy summer and I can't wait for the next.

P.S. To all readers we hope you enjoyed this tale.

ABOUT THE AUTHORS

Eliana Hutson is an 8 year old rising 3rd grader who lives in Harlem, New York. She enjoys traveling, spending time with friends, legos, playing guitar, swimming, volleyball, video games, exploring new cuisines and reading. XXXXX is her 2nd book. She would like to thank her friends from WOL for their constant ideas and support!

Madeleine Ha is an 8-year-old rising 3rd grader at The Dalton School in New York City. In school, her favorite subjects are library, writing, and social studies. Stories of Camp Oakwood is her second book. Her first book, Magical Lives, was published in April 2021. She would like to thank her group of writer friends for always cheering her on and her family for their undying support.

Ruthie Gluck Feder is 9 years old and lives in New York City. She loves cats, hip hop dance, everything theater, her friends, and of course, creative writing. She attends The Dalton School, with her two big brothers, who are super annoying. Ruthie has been attending summer camp in Connecticut since she was one-year-old---and camp is her favorite place on earth.

Samaya Dewan lives in NYC with her Mom, Dad, older sister Sofiya **and** her cavapoo dog Sienna. She is in third grade at the Dalton School. She loves reading, singing, dancing and drawing. She has published one book and this is her second. Her friends are a big part of her life.

Victoria Collett is an 8-year-old New Yorker who loves exploring her city, reading, writing, comedy, and acting. She has had roles on TV shows and on Broadway. She loved writing this book with her friends and is grateful for the encouragement of her family.

Zoe Jovanovic White is an 8-year-old 3rd grader at Dalton. She enjoys athletic pursuits, all the arts -both performing and visual- and above all playing with friends. So far she has authored two books and a couple of screenplays. She would like to thank her dog Sasha for her constant support and share a message with all readers that House 14 Girls rock! She hopes that this book brings joy to whomever reads it.